# A Long, Dark, Grim Road

by
Joseph S. Pulver, Sr.

Lovecraft eZine press

# PRAISE FOR JOSEPH S. PULVER, SR.

". . . I'M GAWPING IN AMAZEMENT, SHAKEN BY PULVER'S EVISCERATING VISION. HE WIELDS LANGUAGE AS A SCALPEL, A THOMPSON SUBMACHINE GUN, AN AXE . . . JOE PULVER CALLS DOWN THE FIRE. JOE PULVER'S THE MAN. HE'S GOT THE POWER."
— LAIRD BARRON, AUTHOR OF *Occultation* AND *The Imago Sequence*

"SOME WRITERS ONE ADMIRERS AND OTHERS MAKE ONE WANT TO DO AS THEY DO, OR TRY. FOR ME, JOE PULVER IS OF THE LATTER TYPE. HIS IMAGINATION IS SO VILE SO MUCH OF THE TIME THAT IT MAKES ME GIGGLE WITH AMAZEMENT. AND THE PROSE SO DEADLY VISIONARY."
— THOMAS LIGOTTI, AUTHOR OF *The Conspiracy Against The Human Race*

"JOE PULVER IS A DARK STAR IN THE MERCILESS COSMOS OF WEIRD FICTION. HIS WORK IS AS BRUTAL AS IT IS BEAUTIFUL."
— W.H. PUGMIRE, AUTHOR OF *The Tangled Muse*

"HIS WORK CATERS TO A LITERARY HUNGER YOU DIDN'T EVEN KNOW YOU HAD, AND DOES IT DARKLY AND DELICIOUSLY."
— MATT CARDIN, AUTHOR OF *Dark Awakenings*

"IF YOU LIKE YOUR PROSE (AND POETRY) HAUNTING, HALLUCINATORY, AND FULL OF HEART, READ JOE PULVER."
— ROBIN SPRIGGS, AUTHOR OF *Diary of a Gentleman Diabolist*

**N**o wine or spirits. No coffee. Tea (the last of it) from our provisions. With goat's milk and no sugar or honey.

Bread—no butter, lard. Goat cheese. From a cast-iron fry pan, meat, I'd wager it was stag (Janning was certain it was not boar), sizzled in lard. Boiled cabbage came out of a pot that could have been 100 years old, a pot that could have been left out and stormbattered by 1000 gales. No salt. No pepper. No spices. (Janning later said, he thought it odd they had no garlic or onions or potatoes, or chickens.) Nothing (on the rough-hewn uneven table) would win a blue ribbon, or a mention in any conversation about tasty. Without a word or a grumble or spitting and not much more than a scowl in our direction, the old man's bent, old wife slapped the meager rations she cooked on chipped old plates and set it before us. We chewed, kept it down.

End of the day's long road. Long road, slowed by ruts, slowed by uneven and the circumstances of mud and rocks. Wet gullies and dry gullies. Long road of dust our horses' hooves threw up, of dust pushed in our faces by the wind. Not a devastating road, but it had moments where it had its brutal on display. No inn, a small dwelling of grey stones that showed its wounds and biting poverty.

The bent old man (bent by a life of ever-repeated consequences) told Janning, the three of us could bed-down in the small wooden structure he called a barn. We did. With three horses (an old black gelding that belonged to the old man and the two of ours that pulled our coach), three noisy goats, half a dozen chickens, and an owl—it watched us for a short time and deciding we were not rats, or tasty, left for the dark wilds of nighted, thick forest. The old man's dog was lucky; he got to stay in the house with the warm-embers of the hearth.

We slept on hay (it was thankfully dry, and insect free), in our coats and hats and gloves. The cold held us fast and we shivered. Janning, our guide and sometimes translator, whispered something that started off sounding like a curse and made its way to sounding like a heated-appeal in the mother tongue, and slept with his American Winchester rifle. Outside in the impossibly-thick blackness, horribly suggestive sounds, not howls or barks, but unnatural *growlings*, snapped and fell, and sour smells, rotten and blatantly graveish, accompanied them. Janning's white-knuckled hands refused to lessen their grip on his American Winchester rifle and he repeatedly mumbled about the *anderen Wölfe* and *der Weg nach Hause*, and the *Graue Blutegel.*

Break of day. Woke. Deeply chilled, but in one piece. Sat inside by the old man's small fire as it struggled to stand tall. What passed for herb tea. Cheese. And a slice of yesterday's bread. No marmalade no sugar no coffee no eggs.

I assisted Janning in hitching our horses to the coach. Brother Sebastiano performed his abrupt task. We did not turn and look upon the bent old man and his old woman.

Stripped of its language and latitude, summer had ended. We rode... the road against us. The sky darkening against us. Trees and dense dark woods, green weed and vine and leave, formless full of secrets, the wilds of impenetrable, about us, bending in to clutch. Threatening forest bent over our coach, against us. Another day, another day in a long string of slow hard days, on dark roads, and everything before us, against *our mission.*

Afternoon was behind us and we had not come upon shelter. My timepiece was firm on the subject, we had ridden for 10 hours and not seen any sign of residence, or the little histories, men, fumbling with science and God and sticks-and-stones, try to leave.

Janning built a small fire and we sat, with our backs against a large boulder, eating from tins. It was a feast of taste in comparison to last night's fare.

Brother Sebastiano, the third member of our company, sat (in the blackness, above us in the driver's seat) with his Holy Cross and American Winchester rifle, and his confidence in the influence of the Saints, watched. Listened to the tangle of night sounds that abounded around us. Prayed. Softly, quietly, passionately.

Another dim morning of dour light in the sky. Another unimportant cottage, a poor farmer's dwelling.

A hard, leathery man, in his 40's, not yet bent, worn but not broken. And at his side (part of and apart), infant in her thin adolescent arms—not in a cradle, not sleeping gently sweetly, smiling up dreaming Mother, not wrapped in soft blankets of bright color in a cradle, child of three or four years of age at her feet (rigid stockstill child same color as her worn shoes), the girl-child that cooked his meals and suffered his bed. (Later, Janning, disgusted in the extreme, spoke of her countenance; she bore the peasant-farmer's look, his shadowgrey coloring of flesh and hair and eye, a cousin, or sister no doubt. "Inbred barbarians. Foul affronts to Holy God.")

He had two sheep and two goats and 4 chickens, a horse and a cart with a broken wheel, a woodpile that would not survive winter. And two perversely-thin cats that rattled with predatory greeds. Grew carrots and Kohlrabi, tomatoes, herbs, and between each row or bunch or struggling plant, weeds, tall, grey, tiptoeing and splitting the fare intended for consumption.

He did not offer us the small comforts of his abode—a thankless place, no pictures, no books, but put us in the barn. In exchange for our silver, he brought us a small loaf of thickly-crusted bread and a small pot of broth with a few potatoes and carrots in it, the smell of it was not inviting. Sebastiano would not eat the fare; he dined on a tin from our provisions. When Sebastiano had finished his small meal he sat by our small fire and began his evening ritual, he prayed and as he begged Holy God to bless our holy charge, he sharpened his blades.

Janning, never parted from it, slept with his American Winchester rifle. I, fully attired and bound in a course blanket, tried to quiet the unthinkable that stirred in the cold night around us and sleep.

Several times I awoke from my brief excursions in sleep (short of breath, but not absent reflections of my fears) to the growlings (and what monstrous thing responded to their terrifying calls) outside. Each time I noted Janning, his immanent fear of damnation and destruction, how tightly he gripped the American Winchester rifle. It was always difficult to tell if Sebastiano, a rigid shape cold and dark as the cold and dark around us, slept, or merely rested with his eyes closed, as he, soundless and hard as an old grave, never moved. And every night when my eyes fell upon Brother Sebastiano in this state of repose, my thoughts went to Brother Carlos Alberto, a true and dutiful servant of Holy God, gone from our company... torn from us—cut—butchered—*savaged*—his soft features, his soft shining eyes, his soft skin—the cascade of cheer and goodwill his boyish smile brought to us.

Cut away.

Damned.

Flesh ripped into silence, ended—but not from our tears.

Brother Carlos Alberto—

Just a boy. Pure. A tender light filled with his unbending love of Holy God and the saints.

Gone. The word is a scar crusted with biting-salt, a

mouth burdened by hunger, a specter fingers cannot touch (even as we see the face that will never again see our face smile or wear agreement).

Gone. Suddenly. The nature of his years, what he preferred, how much he liked sour pickles and was quick to join in laughter... gone. *Taken from us.* He was the youngest among us and filed with granite expectations that Indomitable God would carry our company through any darkness. Three months ago (a warm night, a night that began with nightingales and the math of coupling), Brother Carlos Alberto left the shadows of the out-building we were staying in, went outside to relive himself, and was taken by the other wolves of *Graue Blutegel.*

Carved-up.

A young man, then, a thing... ripped open.

Damned.

Blood spilled. Missing his right hand. Torn, a piece over there, no whole for the grave. He did not even fire a shot from his American Winchester rifle. A spilled scream, half of one. Growlings. A syllable torn from a word's birth. The sound of teeth cutting away. A grunt. Cut—the teeth ripping, ripping forearm and torso ripping shoulder and thigh. He did not even fire a shot from his American Winchester rifle. Bit and bit and bit and bit ripped. No whole to enter Heaven. Part of a snapped thigh bone, no legs. He did not even fire a shot from his American Winchester rifle. No face. He did not even fire a shot. Bowels opened. Blood spilled. Spilled, drop... and stream. Not much of a shape to put in the grave we dug.

Blood spilled three months ago. The youngest of our company torn away, put in this hard uncaring ground, this unholy ground, this terrible ground peace cannot touch. We said prayers over him. Crossed ourselves. Cursed ourselves. An extended silence as we stood there, lamppost-straight on the outside, bent and hollowed inside. Stood, in tears. Last spade of dirt placed on his unmarked grave, we rode away. Didn't turn to look at the purifying blaze and the bodies we left behind— we never do.

Morning, no jewel. Up, involved in the *this* we gripped, not arrows ready for color. We, direct (as a singing voice that will not be dimmed) but not without faults, were about our responsibility.

Janning hitched our road-weary horses, the tack creaked. Sebastiano washed the task from his hands in a wooden pail at the well. I watched, listened, had made sure (wet road, or wind formed by a fist of war, or wobbling from the heat, or breached by cold that will not be brought down by fire, or pleas for mercy) we were packed. Our wheels turned, slowly, over rut and rock. We rode away. Didn't turn to look at the blaze and the bodies we left behind.

We never do.

Never… *after the first time.*

Grey, threatening rain.

We moved forward—a small boat on a large ocean, an ocean with a mouth of thirst, chasing and being chased, giving wrong to wrong. Forward… a tree stands green, it has composed leaves to assert it is here, from need or tingling gestures spoken by life it weaves its pages. Weeds (fresh stubs grasping for height and control and knee-high—many thorned, thin or overgrowth dense) strive; bushes and brambles (many thorned) and plants (head-high and higher) add their splinters to Leviathan—vast, thick, unending. Green. Dark and shadowed. Green. An ocean—a gale unmarked by law, an unabridged shape (that will not be read or buckled to fixed) with Godforsaken deeps, a roaring spell of SELF tingling in the wind, occasionally patterned, occasionally dotted with tiny patches of flowering color. Green that cannot be mapped.

Damnation road. Long hard slow. Dusty, or wet, slow—in the rain with no mind to stop, in the wind (that tears and pushes) with no mind to stop, in the mud (underfoot) that rejected freedom and borders. Our weary brown horse and our weary black horse, urged to pull and pull harder (the tack creaked), were slow. We were not slow to judge. Our hands were not slow to end what was said and lied about (by brutish men converted to Odalric's sinful demonology and the heathen women that freely—*we were certain*—shared their innavigable subsisting). We had no doubts—we were *pure*, Most Holy God aided us in making all decisions, steadied our hands. We were not slow to cleanse the ground with fire. Man with a woman by his side, babies, or children hiding in mother's skirts, we were not slow to spill blasphemers' blood.

Satan has a way with fire.

Sebastiano has a way with it too.

Sebastiano's is no less damning.

Sun up, fighting the greyness. Another slow is born, it decrees struck and staggered for your labors. Leaves flit by like mad wounded birds, strike us in passing. The wind turns the horses' heads. They struggle on—dust, what it pushes at them (in their eyes, in their broad nostrils). Our black horse struggles. Our brown horse struggles. Our black horse is dusty. Our Brown horse is dusty. Up a muddy hill, the wind pushing down, we get out and lead them, tugging a rope. They say nothing as we pull and urge.

We walk half a day, too much of it uphill. We curse—the wind, the road, our horses. We judge—ourselves, curse ourselves. We curse the terrible that is hidden here. The road and the darkening grey sky and our self-worth mock us.

There was smoke on the horizon, thick smoke rising from many chimneys. "A village of blasphemies," Sebastiano said. I could tell he was pleased with the thought of cutting things (throat, and every creek and root and day of thirst, and linen breast) open. The trees thinned. The road was drier, became sturdy, it reflected nothing but was not silent. The wind whispered of ancient black secrets.

Disquieting arrangements of cruelly-bent sticks (that bring to mind winding serpents locked in a hideous and exotic mosaic) and small bones are tied together with exact repeating patterns of rope, they hang from tree branches. The offerings, or representations, warnings perhaps, we know not what they are, shudder and rock in the wind; their movements are deeply unsettling and loathsome. Strikingly similar, fist-size rocks and antlers and small skulls (most are birds skulls) and crudely-woven, little baskets hang in other limbs lining the road; the array is a song of the Devil. We come upon seven stacks of considerable stones on the low side of the road, (Janning spat, "Unholy sentinels."); each formation is crowned with the skull of a scorched-black goat or stag. "The adherents of Odalric and Satan have constructed a corridor of Hell," Sebastiano said, crossing himself. These stone sentinels, primitive affronts to architecture, not built by tradespeople or the sane, are tilted, they should not stand, not with Newton's principles of gravity and this raw, vigorous wind against them, yet they do. In-between each configuration is an unnaturally-large, single grave-mound. Thrust into these mounds are three poles, set in a line. The shortest (and thinness) is closest to the road, the middle pillar is nearly twice its height (and thickness), and the last, again double the height (and span) of the center pole. Atop each sits a nest of gathered sticks and woven long grasses and weeds, each of the three nests were dyed red. Below what we surmise to be some type of nest, or unholy vessel, the poles are wrapped in furs and hides. The most unsettling aspect of these abhorrent totems is the startling actuality that they are faithful duplicates of one another. There is no sign of Our Beloved and Holy Christ or anything of Lord God and his Grace here.

Sebastiano crosses himself and asks God to aid us when we stand face to face with this new gathering of two-footed beasts.

Sebastiano spat. "Another village of unholy servants going nowhere. This land will not permit motion. The wind will not permit it.'

"These demon-processed heathens have tied themselves to Satan and his devil-fiends, and *they* will not permit it."

What had been the road (our path from forested-hours with the dead to questions of latching our harpoons to other shores) became an open field with a tiny cluster of fifteen houses (a tiny cluster of misery, sentenced to participate in evil, where nothing had changed in a hundred years, stained by lifetimes of darkness burning) and a common house nearly in its center. Every grim and weathered residence was an eerie study in disintegration and decay—it was all grey, everything cracked the wind and rain and harsh winters of razor-cold had not been kind to it.

There was no church. These wounded places where the rot and malice of *pagan blackness* is a fist, never have a church.

Pigs. Chickens pecked in circles.

The pigs were bony. The chickens could barely stand.

Goats in a small pen of twisted sticks and cracked, weathered boards.

Horses in an enclosure not suited for large creatures.

A grunt. A glare. No words. A bullring came to mind; we face fume, challenge it.

Two women (experts with the blade and the task they were performing), tall women, resolute women, the older bent from years of hard labor, were butchering an undersize stag.

An arm that ends with a wooden pitchfork. A black boot rests on a spade. An older man coughs; there is illness in his lungs. There is a girl… a wife, a daughter, we do not know. She has very long hair. Brown hair. Uncombed hair. There is a leave trapped in it. She's wearing an old brown coat. It has been repaired and patched many times. She wears a knee-length black cape with a hood that will not stay up and worn black boots. Her handmade brown dress is the wrong size. Her fingernails are dirty and uneven, her hands are rough. Her nose was once broken. There is an uneven 4-inch scar on her left cheek under her brown left eye; it is an old scar that was poorly stitched. Her lips are dry and cracked. The set of her lips and the intensity in her eyes speak of hate. She eats from the field the grasshopper eats in. She has never dreamed of Andromeda, or Rome, or *dear to me*.

There were 17 villagers standing before us. Teeth and heel raggedly, 17 ruined and restitched together time and time again. They could have been the remnants of invaded; they were broken, missing a sliver of ear, missing a thumb, one an eye. Other scars, echoing shadows and the cost of starved—its rage, its pockets trying to outrun stasis. 17 open mouths and an enormous silence. Pale faces—dreary, mouth hands stripped of hope—slipping, fading… drained, dreary. Eyes nervous, some rheumy, eyes that had seen trouble blistering, eyes of repulsed by and temper; you could measure them out (the corpse-sound they unraveled) as spoonfuls of miles that could not be saved. A couple, taller than the others, closer to us than the others. Her dim eyes are the color of this grim land under the dark sky, the color of the voiceless bog. His glared. Hers are grey, ash-grey, ruined. His are grey, ash-grey, ruined. Grey, the weather of their ruined hearts. Grey the endless sky. Grey the hovel-wombs that crumble around them. Grey the desperate caress in spells of rain. Grey that touches and overruns night and day and every gesture and gallery of tedium. Some let their hands hang at their sides, others cross their arms. Half of the gathering is too thin, and looks ready to split at the seams. There was not an oracle in the bunch.

They look at us. Eye to eye. We look at them. Face to face. Loathing. Fear. No good. Temper with anger at its left. What is between us cannot be ignored.

They hate.

We brim with hate… for them. And for their dreadful master.

Dreary. Subsistence—mouth, hands stripped of hope—dreary, worn. Sun out or hidden or banned from the day's sky, the land, its harsh-faced people, are grey. Dreary. Sick, every horse, every chicken and pig and goat, sick, every posture and *maybe* that means *never again*. Sick, every bloodshot eye that falls upon us and would choke us, murder us, connect us to crashing ill; laden with grim we are, but we will not be derailed. Sick mouths, sick eyes, foul hearts, made dreary and *unclean* by evil's liniments. Banned from peace, from mercy, from the power of the Saints, from the *Goodness* of Sweet Christ. Dreary. Unclean screaming their evil lies—fiends, vile dolts moored in squalor—scourge and transgression (it rakes and stains, sends Satanic arcs of witchery to dislocate our balance)—plague, rank, demon-pierced grasped by a name that only brings death—sinners filth consecrated in *Filth* that torture Holy—

Finally a voice, dry blunt unfriendly. "Where are you bound?"

"To Moscow, on a mission for our master. We hoped to find a meal and beds for the night. As you can see, our horses are weary. The road is taxing."

I added. "We can pay with silver."

There was a corner with an uneven board floor in a common house, we could sleep there, near the small hearth. No beds, but we could get a meal, drink homemade potato vodka. We did. I did, a sip against the cold, Janning did. Brother Sebastiano would touch nothing they produced.

Outside in the impossibly-deep indigo, solid as cast-iron, foulsome sounds, packed unnatural *growlings*, snapped and fell, and the sounds of clawed-things-that-slay *barked*, as they moved back and forth around us. Sour smells, rotten and blatantly graveish, accompanied them. Janning whispered about the *anderen Wölfe* and *der Weg nach Hause*, and the *Graue Blutegel*, cursed Odalric and Clithanus and Satan, and crossed himself repeatedly.

We spend a second day among them (resting the horses, we said, as we handed them another silver coin). They were slow, dreary, went about their sluggish routines, farming—scratching in the hard dirt, wood gathering, hunting, slowly, by rote. Three women gathered at the well early and brought buckets of water to every house. Two men with bows slipped into the forest; fearing possible skullduggery, I was quick to draw Brother Sebastiano's attention to the action.

Though we cursed it and prayer for it to be swept to other districts, the abrasive wind did not stop.

Three men dig with simple wooden tools. One yells at the pigs, curses them.

Near the tree-line, the goats, bony, ill-looking, graze on graying weeds.

We see very few birds. This is so unlike my boyhood home in Tuscany.

No dogs. We had not seen a dog in weeks.

*This is so unlike my boyhood home in warm beautiful*

*Tuscany.*

The wind, our ever-present assailant in this inhospitable furnace of damnation, did not stop. Against our words it rushes in. Besets us. There is no slipping out of it. It swirls. It bites, morning afternoon wildly lashes. It claws and rakes and pushes dust and dirt in our faces. It's black-hearted as villainy and often as cold as the winter Northmen endure. The wind did not stop. No beginning. No next follows pause. No cease, opened by will or nature, places its hand to filter the flow. It is as solid as night, thick as the misshapen forest monster that floods over us. The wind is a steady river that cuts through the day. And we, our every act and obligation, are shut-up in it.

So few birds, no dogs, further proof of the ancient foulness that corrupts this unchecked land.

The children do not come outside to play. Sebastiano says he's counted over a dozen, but we do not hear them. More than a dozen children and no laughter or squabbles over procession, no hunger-fueled beseeching? Everything here is unnatural.

Three men, scarred and filth-encrusted, chop wood from a very large pile, two other men, bony, ill-looking (with faces of those lost souls locked away in madhouses for their unnaturalness), carry it to the houses.

A woman, surely, impossibly, not as elderly as her wrinkled countenance portrays, comes out of one of the tiny stone houses. She has black splinters for teeth and a cataract has blinded one eye. The longer one looks upon her, the more one feels she is as old as a work of medieval stone given grotesque suffering by this cruel, unholy place. She carries a crudely-woven basket of briar vines. In its black bowl there are small pieces of rope she tied into exotic knots—each one is the same. She walks to the treeline and nails a knotted talisman of *Graue Blutegel* (an act only described and shown in *The Black Manuscript of Odalric*) to a tree, and repeats her action. She performs this activity until the basket is empty then she returns to the house and refills the basket; the afternoon is giving way to darker shadings of sky before she ceases her task. The wind did not stop, or ease. It and the inexorably grim landscape grind at discipline and intent.

I thought about food. Salami, from bountiful *Genoa*. Pork and bread, the smell of warm loaves. Chianti. *Pici*. Mushrooms and olive oil. And honey and garlic and lamb. Basil, and my mother's *ribollita*.

I miss home—*Rome*—and the comforts, the streets where good men and good women walk, constructive expressing, and expressing myself with good company. Company with good ears and laughs happily, company that permits strength deep down and believes in the power of comedies. I miss the church. God and all His Bright Angels know how I miss it, the faces in the pews, Vatican Hill, the *Baptism of Christ* on the Northern wall of the Sistine Chapel, *The Creation of Adam. Deus, in adiutorium meum intende. Domine, ad adiuvandum me festina. Gloria Patri, et Filio, et Spiritui Sancto. Sicut erat in principio, et nunc et semper, et in saecula saeculorum. Amen. Alleluia*—

Wind. It puts your head down, keeps it there. The wind, this sick wind corrupted by *The Destroyer*, did not stop, its granite brings harm to my memories. It mocks me.

Almost no one spoke to us.

They all watched us.

The third day was a bitter repeat of the second. Janning clutched his American Winchester rifle. Brother Sebastiano dreamed of the fire that destroys. I thought about food and the Grace of God and all His Bright Angels. I said a prayer for Brother Carlos Alberto, a true and dutiful servant of Holy God, gone from our company... *torn from us*—cut—butchered—savaged—his soft features, his soft shining eyes, his soft skin—the cascade of cheer and goodwill his boyish smile brought to us. Brother Carlos Alberto, who would never see Rome again. Just a boy. A tender light, filled with his unbreakable love of Holy God and the saints.

17 ash-grey villagers. They looked at us. Eye to eye. We looked at them. Face to face. What was between us could not be ignored.

We watched. We counted. 17.

17 heathens, demons carved and slithering within them.

Planned.

There would be blood spilled, shots fired from our American Winchester rifles. A spilled scream, half of one. A syllable torn from a word's birth. Blades in play that bit and bit and bit and bit, ripped bowels open. Blood sprayed. Spilled, drop and drop and drop. There would be blood on our hands.

Sebastiano said, "To-morrow." We waited.

Morning put no golden jewel in the sky. Up, involved in the *this* we gripped, firm as arrows deployed. Straight, spirited-lark fast, unswerving shots into hearts. Throats cut. A cartridge finds a leg, another an eye. Gasps. Groans. Shouting we are quick to silence. Arcs of a blade grabbing flesh. None rise to their feet. We, direct as committed talons biting deep, concluded our responsibilities.

Men. Women. The silent children. Bodies in a pile. Livestock left where we felled it.

Janning hitched our horses. Sebastiano washed the task from his hands in a wooden bucket at the well. I watched, listened, had made sure we were packed, tied-down. We rode away, the tack of our horses creaked. Didn't turn to look at the blaze and the breathless bodies we left behind.

We never do.

A day on the road. Grey, threatening rain. The rough uncompromising wind pushes dust and dirt and loose leaves into our brown horse's eyes, the rough uncompromising wind gusts dust and dirt and unfastened leaves into our black horse's eyes. Wind, that must contain teeth suited only to deliver pain, swirls and gusts and slaps the broad nostrils of our horses with dust and dirt. We urge them on. They struggle. Up a short steep hill. Skirting a lifeless grey bog. Down a long slow hill. Through a muddy creek bed. Over ruts and rocks. Our brown horse strains. Our black horse strains. The tack creaks. The only variant in the scouring uncompromising wind is how much cold and moisture it holds from hour to hour. We move slowly, pushing, pulling, urging, in wind—chisel wild as fire or blizzard's maw that intends to devour. Late afternoon we come upon 3 houses. They, ash-grey dreary, mouth and hands stripped of hope—harsh-faced grey people, stand in front of their hovels worn and frayed, offering *poor me* eyes. Liars! Villains, poisonous serpents with human faces. With the new morning, we drag them from the decaying constructions where they fester, and swiftly, we dismember and burn.

Night. Again. All those agains of *last night*, molded by the forces of the persistent absolute of the others, forced upon hands and lips and eyes that would stretch and turn away and gladly wander and adapt to flowers or sun-warmed skies frequented by blue and sunning larks. The black thicket, *night*, briar, taker, smothering shape and molding sound. Not empty, full as funeral. Same as a hundred nights black, same black, groping, same lack of comforting—no hand reveals carefully, same dome of terrors. Erect. Not empty.

Ancient moon (an aphrodisiac to some) with a hunter's face. Chitterings in the dancing blackness beyond our small campfire's weak bay of light. Denied stars by the dense overhanging of wild branches, we sat and waited for light to mark the sky and allow our eyes images.

Surrounded by this pressing estate of *Immortal Wickedness*, I smoked my pipe, hoped a way back home—*to sweet, beautiful Rome*—could be found at the end of this long dark road.

Wet spring thundering and spreading its vines and briars, wet that turned ruts to pits of thick mud persistent mud, wet that denied fire and kept you saturated, dismantled pace, and summer's animal heat and flitting biting insects and chilled nights and sharp wind, each furl of pressing misfortune that vowed to halt the forward we sought, decayed farm house to grim farmer shack, we'd been in this region of blasphemies and dreadfulness for 8 months. 8 months without a proper bed or a suitable meal at a clean table. 8 months tangled and stripped in this no man's land anointed in the coils of madness and hissing with the tongue of the Grey Leech. 8 months being paced and watched by the *other wolves*. 8 months without the cut and alignments of humanity in this season of blood. 8 months in this hell, damned and assailed, without the golden pleasant of the Roman sun and the lucid shapes and colors of Italy's perfumed flowers... and charming swans, and sweetly smiled and fat and new fruit that gave song to the heart and blessed Holy Crosses being worn by the delicate.

Silver crucifix in hands that moved as tongues committed, Brother Sebastiano sat praying, his words terrible fangs promising funeral to the monstrous, and to every unholy adherent of Odalric's plague. Twice I heard him name Clithanus, curse him. Heard him curse the mage, Odalric, once Clithanus' apprentice, who, when Clithanus turned from the dark path and denounced his beliefs, returned to this dark region, his homeland, with a sinful treatise of Satan-spawned wickedness culled from parts of the *Black Confessions*. Returned with the leaves of summoning pagan monsters. Odalric, Satan's black-hearted servant, returned with his *Black Manuscript* to cast out Christianity and restore Satan's demon-fiends in this pagan land.

"Heathen demons. Satan-spawned wickedness carved and slithering within them."

The ancient demonology, *The Confessions of Clithanus the Monk*, spoke of a giant black-skinned demon in a black cloak of black stars that walked the *Barren Meadows Between the Stars*; it said he sometimes walked the earth as a faceless man; Brother Sebastiano, who has studied the ancient text and many, many others, said the Black Man was a mask of Lucifer, fallen from Heaven and forever condemned to roam the blackest deeps. It detailed ancient sea-monsters with unnamable hungers, glorified giants that descended celestial staircases to conduct ambitions no human authority or inquisitor's invention could turn, much less suppress. It contained unholy rites and spells, unholy prayers and unholy offerings, and revealed dark secrets of dead lost cities that could be rebuilt, and foulsome histories covered by the destructive dust of ages. Made and unmade, crisis and damnation, were put on the pages of *The Black Manuscript of Odalric*. Poison its every word and unholy diagram. And the black book spoke of the Thin People of the great northern forests and the Grey Leech and his children, the Other Wolves. With the wicked secrets of the unclean book, the foul, grey people of this hell-spawned territory had summoned up *anderen Wölfe* and *der Weg nach Hause*, and the *Graue Blutegel*. We heard the enemy at night; saw the decay and rancid Nemesis smeared on this land of blight when the grey light's tenure looked around.

Sebastiano cursed everything externally. I cursed everything internally. Janning mumbled and gripped his American Winchester rifle tighter. And we rode on in the rain.

Raining. Rigid. Deep.

Acutely.

It rained yesterday. Rained the day before. Again and again with no breaks or moment where you hope for another reality, the one where pause begins to swirl in your thoughts. Unmerciful rain that did not sleep through the night, or allow you to. Unmerciful rain… that dominated the land, that dominated the trees, that (full of immensities) would not be pushed to a distance that can't explode in this space. Unmerciful rain. Rain… again and again washing all patience from the world.

Rain.

Acutely.

Dependant on nothing, perhaps diabolic.

Overbearing overwhelming grimrain driven by grimwind exhausting rain.

When the rain stopped the wind brought unmerciful cold.

Strange, night with no fox prowling and gathering.

Strange, day, open, full of uninhibited sun colliding with the eye, yet few daybirds—even ravens and crows, fewer still when darkness returns, bats. Few boar. Fewer still, stag. Yet the creeks and small lakes and slow-moving rivers were teeming with marble trout and catfish and pike (which we often caught and ate to augment our provisions), and many, oddlookingcreatures that seemed fitted together from differing species of fish, crustaceans, and octopi. The further we moved from the realm and ages of men, their numbers increased. Once we had moved into the eastern low county, we pulled hard-shelled monsters (of about 60 cm) with featherlike appendages from the inky deeps of the rivers. Sebastiano did not contemplate the mysteries of their creation, whatever their story, it began with some ceremony roused by Satan himself. We would eat the pike and catfish, but these hardshell creatures we did not consume. Like so many other things here, we burned them.

This is an evil land.

Strange worms long and flattened and illness-grey, were in some of the places we bed down. They'd find ways into your pockets or under your shirt while you slept. The oily coating they were greased with greatly-irritated our skin. We ground them under heel or tossed them upon the white-hot embers of our struggling campfires.

This is an unclean land.

A grim land of sin.

They grow weeds bent with turmoil here. Fertilize them with evil and the autumnstillness-laced tapestry the wind brings. They grow weeds here, grave-incense weeds. Weeds that don't own or travel the road. Hideous weeds that see no fare thee well, that grant no fare thee well. Weeds surrounded by collapse, weeds that thirst for sour.

Weeds and rain and wind and ever-returning night.

Sleep. (No fat, warm mattress, no down, no quilt with the power of snug.) All too briefly in a dream, a starless mane, bitten, licked by snakeshapes that spilled orgies of silence and sorrows until my mother's voice called me to shore. Awake, the howling, barking, chittering outside (it rang in my ears like perverted chuckling), ripped me from the many comforts of my mother's kitchen. Sleep with no pleasure in it. Brief clumps of fitfulness shredded by distress and compounded by diabolic and implausibly-faceted shadows. They flit, arc and scuttle around each other in some celebratory witches' dance. Dreams gone, I stand in nightmare, in mud of organic matter and blood, my mother's face shaken by agony (all her humility gone, the bonfire of her abundant love *gone*), her imploring eyes begging this helpless son, as what her cancer wrought smolders within her. And as my mother (filled only with the language of pain) weeps and whimpers His (invading) Wolves laugh; their elongated snouts lean in and awaiting the feast, drool over the rotting meat covering her thin weakened bones. One hundred praying cardinals and bishops surrounded my poor mother's deathbed. Each held a Holy Cross blessed by the Holy Father and an American Winchester rifle. One hundred dead bishops and cardinals now ring her deathbed, a large chunk of flesh and muscle pins a fingerless-hand to the carpeted floor near my feet, a head that now appears to be attached to an ankle rests near my learned mentor, Bishop Ramazzotti. He was disemboweled— crudely-gutted—*by teeth*, tearing snapping teeth... and my dear friend, His Eminence Cardinal Guglielmo Massaia, a sweet and humble servant of Holy God loved by all who he blessed with his kindheartedness and concern, is a profusion of laboratory specimens scattered by deranged intents. Each blessed Holy Cross has been splintered; the barrel of each American Winchester rifle has been twisted. Another night of nightmare-racked periods of sleep, auto-de-fes of loss and hurt and blood.

*Where is warm*?

Blood behind us. Blood in front of us.

Sin in every rock, in every hovel that burns with hunger as cold as the Unclean Blackness between the stars. Sin in every village of devils that would nail Holy to another cross.

The road . . . Barn: hay and shit. Dirtfloor. Cobwebs above. A pitchfork and a shovel. A wooden pail. A wooden wheelbarrow. The horse tack is old cracked. No fire. A wooden toolbox, hammer, hatchet. An axe. Coils of rope— enough to hang their shells from a high tree . . . There are no graves. Sebastiano says they eat their dead . . . Rain. Cold (an expanding fact), the wind is a razor . . . We poison their wells. Leave them for the wind to fill . . . Head down, forcing yourself into the wind . . . *Anderen Wölfe* of the *Graue Blutegel* howling, prowling... for flesh and bone *and soul* . . . No Holy Church bright and pure. No hint of Holy God . . . Rolling fog . . . A scythe by a doorway . . . Hard grey *slow to the grave*. Weathered. Unwashed. Unclean. Day drags dimming light over the horizon. The night comes brings colder cold. Shapes come and go, the moon comes and goes, shadows take on new shapes . . . Broken windowpanes. An abandoned house

. . . The wind does not ease . . . *The monsters here are aware . .  
. Forward in the effects of a grey dream . . . They rise, dress  
work eat their meager rations. They sleep. We take motion  
from them . . . She sits. Silent. Sows, stitch—the needle's to and  
fro, stitch—the needle's to and fro, stitch—the needle's to and  
fro—the needle's to and fro. She, a hard shape with no  
complexities, sits. Says nothing . . . Another darkness settles  
over us . . . Night, huddled close to our fire, dread in our  
hearts, our American Winchester rifles in our hands loaded . . .  
Night, starless filled with cold rain and billowy mists . . . Night,  
sorrow and rage—elements we believe, shock—nocturnal  
processions (things woven of night fever that sing too much)  
filled with damning interactions. We do not share stories. Not  
one of us recites a poem, in the fist of this cold damp mountain,  
not one of us tries to recall one. I smoke the last of my tobacco.  
In our blankets we sit shivering . . . Grey light fills the morning  
sky. The wind whips by. The leaves sheared from stunted,  
gnarled trees strike us . . . Fear. Fear, in shape in shadow, of no  
light in the world, of failing, exhausting fear, its stench, the  
urges of the doom yelling in your stomach . . . "Kyrie, eleison."  
. . . "Christ, have mercy." . . . The long, dark, wet, grim road .  
. . Our road—  
    The tack of our horses creaks . . .  
    The sky was empty, grey. Night fell. No little boy's or  
tender-hearted man's *how I wish* arises, the stars above hold  
only bad memories. Under a substantial outcropping of rock we  
build a fire. Twenty paces beyond it, we built a second, a  
bonfire. The absolute-blackness beyond the illumination of our  
fires' flickering breath is saturated with the voicings and  
movements of creatures set only to devour. Pants. Tricklings.  
Whispers, skitters, sharp barks and rustling, howls, I shudder  
think of the forms and shapes I am unable to look upon.  
"Night's hunters stir," Sebastiano says. I press my back firmly  
against the expansive wall of rock we camp under. Janning, eyes  
closed as he attempts slumber, mumbles something  
unintelligible; we'll sleep in shifts, two American Winchester  
rifles ready to speak against the unkind bearing of any assailant.  
Our holy crosses, blessed by His Eminence Cardinal Guglielmo  
Massaia, reflect the fire's radiance. I have a headache brought on  
by anxiety and strained eyes, it keeps me from sleep. Should I  
return to Rome, I shall have to, yet again, confess to my  
confessor, His Eminence Cardinal Guglielmo Massaia, the  
stewing fear in my belly was stronger than the strength I sought

after in the Holy Cross. Weak grey light finally arrives and we ride on. I briefly drowse in the back of our coach.

Two hovels of stone and wood facing each other from opposite sides of the road. Grey, cracked houses on inhospitable plots of grey earth, even the weeds struggle. There is a face in the window on the lowside of the road. A woman's face. A grey face—its stench. It does not move. Cold dead minutes not fit for memory and more minutes (lifeless wastes) shed, its expression does not change, no variation is uttered. We call out and no one answers. Nothing stirs. We wait and call out again, louder. The woman's grey face does not move. The pelting gloom of the grave, its eyes on every creature of this dreary to and fro, grins. Her face is a desert, her mouth is a desert. Her eyes are shadows of all that was lost. This hour and the last, the skullface framed by the weathered grey casement does not move, will not reply to our calling. The other window, the cracked and grey one on the hardscrabble highside of the road, mirrors its twin. Its captured face does not move, will not answer. What do these somnambulists stare at, some hollow BLACKNESS that dreams of filling its emptiness? Is it leashed to the *Graue Blutegel's* vampiric suckling? I have rapped on the doors, my knuckles thunder. Sebastiano has looked around, Janning walked the treeline. We've seen no men, no children, not a horse or a pig or a chicken or a goat, there are no stories here—here, in the vast *none*, is only funeral. Inside we leave them bloody, burning.

Day, what passes for it here.

Janning hitched our road-weary horses, the tack creaked. I watched, listened, had made sure (wet road, or wind formed by a fist of war, or wobbling from the heat, or breached by cold that will not be brought down by fire, or pleas for mercy) we were packed. Our wheels turned, slowly, over rut and rock. We rode away. Didn't turn to look at the blaze we left behind.

We never do.

The road. Hard every hour.

The tack of our black horse creaked.

The wind. Spread like a predator.

The tack of our brown horse creaked.

Long morning on the road, slowed by uneven and the circumstances of mud and rocks. The rough uncompromising wave of Satan-wind pushes dust and dirt and loose leaves into our brown horse's eyes, the rough uncompromising wind gusts dust and dirt and unfastened leaves into our black horse's eyes. Wind, that must contain teeth suited only to deliver pain, swirls and gusts and slaps the broad nostrils of our horses with dust and dirt. We urge them on. They struggle. The tack of our black horse creaked. Up a short steep hill. Skirting a lifeless grey field of grave mounds. Down a long slow hill. The tack of our brown horse creaked. Through a muddy creek bed. Over ruts and rocks. Our brown horse strains. Our black horse strains. The tack creaks and creaks. The only variant in the scouring uncompromising wind is how much cold and moisture it holds from hour to hour. We move slowly, pushing, pulling, urging, in wind wild as inferno or blizzard's maw that intends to devour. Long afternoon on the road, slowed by uneven and the circumstances of mud and rocks. Dust and dirt. The rough wind gusts.

A hovel. The straw of its roof needs repair; its door is missing a board. Two brittle, weathered crones reside here; they smell of shit and are covered in open sores. Signs of the labors of their elbows and hands, servants of Death's reverie, are smeared on every flat surface here. No traveler's fare offered by the viper-tongues, toothless mouths foam, coarsely piping meadows of hatred upon us. We spill blood from corrupt shores of chest and throat, spill the contents of their cauldron.

Nothing here can be redeemed!

Janning will put all to the torch in the morning.

I am jarred awake. Janning (there is no trace of peace or calm on his scarred and bearded face), in the center of the floor near the tiny hearth and the edges of its tiny outstretched fluttering fire, bleeding nightmares, moans. Underneath his military-hard quiet, in his head and fistsolidheart, Brother Sebastiano gathers his *bad* in the cold air. I can feel it ripple, soon his deliberate blades and the merciless-consequences of the cartridges in his American Winchester rifle will hurt and lay waste again.

Quickened breath sounds in the candlelit hovel. I feel tightness in my stomach. My throat is dry; it bears the taste of fear.

Outside, not turned or acknowledged by the rushing wind, is the masking blackness of night and its suffocating night-acres. Beyond these crude stone walls, deviltry—menace, satanicdeep sataniccold—crammed with miles and layers that hunt. There are other *things* in this predatory night; foul-shapes that can transform, things with the faces and hideous bodies of nameless devils, foul-things marked by demonic portents; malevolence not recorded by Father Sebastien Michaelis and Francis Barrett.

The tongue of the abyss licks this room. It seeks form and mind, color and landscape. Knowing only darkness and its dreams, it sends the dance of its furnace toward every curve and ripple of our being.

There is a homeless beetle on the filthy floor of this stone cage; its silhouette on the floor is mindless of nemesis. Like our own, its path is thunder, its legs, slaves—punctured by silence, colliding with the slaughterhouse, working over crack and dustymound of badlanddirt, do not know straight or escape.

Blatantly graveish, the barking of the *anderen Wölfe* call to the *Graue Blutegel*. They would devour this land, climb, stretch, gallop from these blackmountainsides of heathen-born madness all the way to Sweet Rome, and tear it apart.

The beetle slides into a deep crack in the hearth. For a moment I see my mother's hearth bathed in vibrant sunshine and *a ruin lizard sunning itself on the bright yellow wall above. My grip tightens on my American Winchester rifle; I must get home. I must see men,* celebrations, and the history of Grace again. I open my eyes and see Brother Sebastiano, his expression is a series of storms that must kill, must silence all of Satan's lice.

"The cursed light of this unholy realm will arrive soon." Sebastiano says.

Satan created all manner of demons. They walk the land—this grim evil land of blight and boundless horrors. In ancient times before they were locked away, they fell upon the Earth from the stars. These demons, far greater than the leviathans hunted by whalers who sail from midnight to midnight to profit from the harpoon-unleashed, roiled in the seas. They sailed the skies. We cleanse what we can. With blades. With bullets. With fire. With hearts and vows in service to the LORD.

A stone hovel. One horse. Two bony goats. A dreary man bent from repeated labors, a miserable grey man inside and out. Not in service to the LORD! *Not in service to the LORD!* Damned, no glimmer of hope, no life churning inside of him. His wife, wounded, grey and dreary as her much-older spouse. Harsh-faced, worn, the pair of grey *pagan sinners.* There is a boy of 10 or 12, and 3 smaller children, not more than babes. All appear sickly, ash-grey. They act simple, guiltless. They have no food to offer, no barn for us overnight in. We are not tricked by their masquerade, we take Satan's unclean children right there. Janning shoots the man in the face with his American Winchester rifle. Sinners' blood spilled. Sebastiano slits the woman' throat. Spilled, drop and drop... and scarlet stream. In terror, the heathen children stand brittle, immobile. Then our medicine put them down. We will burn the bodies and their hovel in the morning.

Hard frost burns hungry-green from the trees. Browns and yellows and reds are the colors of the rotting foliage now. Bushes are shorn. This hellish cold will not be contained or pushed away. Evermore overbearing, the wind punishes us, slows us. The hills are steeper, the ruts and gullies deeper. Though we serve the LORD, the road, long road, bumpy road, slowed by rocks and potholes, slowed by uneven, will not allow forward.

Our provisions are low and our coach is a poor conveyance in this region sore-unclean, as we stare at the arrival of November's bitter talons. We are headed home, to sweet Rome to winter, to report and confer, to restore our energies for next year when we again return to assist Brother Sebastiano with his holy battle against the *Graue Blutegel* and the *anderen Wölfe.*

The road. Hard *every hour.* The tack of our black horse creaks. All day. The wind. Piercing. Late-autumn cold laden with moisture. Spread like a predator. The tack of our brown horse creaks. All day. The tack creaks . . . The wind slaps us with a tree of dry, loose leaves, stripped of life's rhyme. A forest and the brittle-scraps of a dying field follow, sand dances in the swirling battery.

The difficult road. By my reckoning, midday.

A small muddy creek has overrun its shallow banks and spilled over the road. I climb down and test the hazard for depth and rocks, or washout, with a long stick. Janning also climbs down and together, we urge and tug our horses through the ankle-deep water. We cross the wet expanse slowly. Up a short hill. Down into a dark gulley. We slide under the dark canopy of high interwoven branches and dense broadleaf. Trees that rise up three-or-more-times-the-height of a tall man before they sprout a limb, not one is straight, or a leave cradle a very large grove of hard ground embedded with rocks. There are many split and fallen boughs here. A broad smear of shadows merges with deeper jagged shadows. There is a doorway in the dark haze under the dark trees in this secluded patch. The slate-black doorway is too large for the small shack, twice too large.

This is a bad place, a coffin at the bottom of a hill.

This is a bad place.

*Satan is Lord here.*

The immobile scent of ancient corruption is heavy in this gulley. Breathing the heavy stale-air that grips the murky plot we stand in is like taking nails into your lungs.

After gulping several times, Janning summons his voice and calls out.

Silence.

Sebastiano squints into the deep hazy shadows.

We wait.

Janning calls out again. Louder.

Silence.

Our American Winchester rifles are ready to hurry breath to dead.

The door of the small shack finally opens. A grey shape emerges, we three, strain to define it, as it swells in the air. I stare in disbelief, the shadows in direct contact with the shape become lighter, it is absorbing them, they fuel its inhuman expansion.

"Witch," Sebastiano hisses softly.

I find myself shocked that Sebastiano does not put her down immediately.

"Woman, we seek food and a place to bed down for the night. We have silver," Janning says.

The old woman, old crone, bent, slow, let us in her small dwelling of grey boards and stones. She is tiny again. She was missing an eye. The other, too blue—uncomfortably blue, rattled with clarity, it was an eye that would look you in the mouth and quarrel, offer to pin you to the quickest form of death the sum of her demonic thoughts could conjure for you. Her face was a horde of harsh wrinkles; small insects could have resided in the deeps, other things, too, I did not want to know of their "possibilities". What remained of her hairline had receded and thinned and was now a crown of small caps of grey and yellowy-white wisps. Her nose was wide—two faces wide, bent just under the eye, broken more than once. The wrinkle-stitched corners of her mouth are downturned. Hazard walks across her brow. Throat, shoulders (one is much lower than its opposite, the arm and hand attached to it, much slower), and chest had lost their mass; it had slid down and accumulated in her flabby midsection, giving her a pear-shaped look. She is ribs and bones and forces that will not be locked out by a door or the desires of *good* sane men, and this trickster clothed in the skin of a weary hag is nothing charming.

I had stood outside; certain this was a small place. Yet, its interior—unevenly walled, is a large rectangle with a very lofty ceiling. There are many small hooks above our heads. Suspended from each hook is a gut-string, noosed, small cluster of dry plants or unrecognizable roots, woven within and between is a community, the dance floors and patterns, of spiders. Several wax lights and the small fire of her hearth manipulate the light and air in this place of deceptive shadows. If there were color here in the variant shades of grey and blackness, if it could crawl in and cling to a wooden cup or to her bedding, it would drive the observer mad.

There is very little furniture inside her dwelling. In the four years I have traveled in these provinces of unholiness and blazing bitterness, I have never seen a desolate shack or decaying hovel appointed with a single comfort. (Yet, there is one other observation that remains constant; disquieting arrangements of cruelly-bent sticks, that fill the mind with images of winding serpents locked in a hideous and exotic mosaic, and small bones are tied together with exact repeating patterns of twine or gut-string, hang from the broughs. The offerings, if that is what they are, shudder and rock in the wind; their movements are deeply unsettling and loathsome. Beside them, fist-size stones and antlers and small skulls and crudely-woven, little baskets hang from other limbs along the road.)

We sit on two unsteady benches at a rough-hewn, uneven table, while this creature-we-are-to-believe-is an old woman placed a very small cabbage, 3 unpeeled potatoes (that look like knots or fists), and 2 small carrots in an iron-pot that could have been left out in 1000 gales. She stands with her small-back to us, over her pot, (tapping her wooden spoon on the rim exactly four times each time she taps it), I cannot tell if she's humming some part of a queerly-foreign folk melody or chanting; it is not a pleasant singsong she issues. There is an elongated note at the end of every noisy, buzzing phrase, she coughs out. In reaction to her utterance, Sebastiano's fingers settle on the handle of his knife. Boiled came out of the pot. Janning and I try to eat. Sebastiano broke the silence of our hesitant lips and tongues with his sudden, condemning knife and her response to its tempest, her death-rattle. I stood, looked at what was done and spilled-out on the table and a small pooling on the hard-dirt of the floor.

Sebastiano incinerates everything that will burn. There is more to do in this ill land, the *Old Work* flourishes here. Blast of wind… we ride on—

Another house of pain and lies and acts against Holy God. Unholy, inhuman acts. Abundant unholy horrors. Evil to destroy. Children and maws to silence, to kill. Another pyre to singe Satan's fingers. Sebastiano glories in it. Janning seeks revenge for his devastation—the savage murder of his beloved and their infant twins—his hatred is 3 years old, 3 years hard, 3 years unquenched. We kill and burn and ride on.

Dust… and more dust. Wind and merciless cold.

Wind. Unceasing unmerciful wind.

The tack creaks.

Another shack. Another pair of bent grey blasphemers. Our American Winchester rifles and the torch are tempests that speak for God.

Dust… and more dust. Wind and merciless cold.

Wind.

The tack creaks.

And another hut of foul blasphemers. Our American Winchester rifles and the torch are tempests that speak for God.

Dust… and more dust, it gets in our horses' nostrils. Wind, it turns our horses' heads, and merciless cold.

The tack creaks.

We torched 5 residences today. Incinerated 3 yesterday. One hut was the quarters of a pair of albinos, brother and sister caught rutting, he had her bent over a tree trunk near their woodpile, and she bellowed with foul-joy as her skeletal-rump thrust to meet the thrusts of his foul-root. The cartridges from our American Winchester rifles fed on them; there was little left of their heads—faces, for the flames to feed on when it rose up. Inside the shack of this pair of demon-worshipers we found proof of witchery, of their devotion to Satan, a shelf with handwritten pages, copied from the *The Black Manuscript of Odalric*. Poison words, spells and chants, unholy diagrams and crude pictorials of blasphemous Satan-spawn that conquered sea and forest, desert waste and sky. And on every cluttered page of dry paper, the demonology spoke of the *anderen Wölfe* and *der Weg nach Hause*, and the *Graue Blutegel*. Every foulsome page was stained with wicked, disquieting secrets and unholy ceremonies taken to heart by the abhorrent inhabitants of this

Hell-infected territory. Amid decay and rancid we burned. Watched it all burn. Blast of wind... we rode on—

End of the day's long road. I have been at this for four years now. Long road, slowed by ruts, slowed by miserable events and the circumstances of mud and rocks. Janning joined me two years ago. Wet gullies and dry ravines. Sebastiano has accompanied us for the past two years as well. Long road of dust our horses' hooves threw up, of dust pushed in our faces by the wind. We three have gazed upon horrors, a devastating road; it displays everything vile and unholy. We have eaten dust... and more dust, and have been chewed upon and beaten by the merciless cold. No inn, a small dwelling of grey stones that showed its wounds and biting poverty. A long road. Grim. Deadly. Dire; I was the only one to return to Rome that first year—the *anderen Wölfe* took my companions, Francis Woodward, Brother Salvatore, Brother Luigi, cut away, damned, flesh ripped into silence, ended—but not from my tears and prayers. Sky full of grey. Wind and dust, the acts of destruction, no pleasant dreams, monsters and ancient darkness. Moments of hopelessness. The wind, our ever-present assailant in this inhospitable furnace of damnation, did not stop. Against our words it rushes in. Besets us. There is no slipping out of it. It swirls. It bites, morning afternoon wildly lashes. It claws and rakes and pushes dust and dirt in our faces. The wind did not stop. There is beginning or middle to it. No cease places its hand to filter the flow. It floods over us. The wind is a steady river that cuts through the day. And we, our every act and obligation, are shut-up in it. I have been at this for four years now. Break of day. Awake. Deeply chilled, but in one piece. We ride on. Another dim morning of dour light in the sky. Another dour, weathered dwelling stands before us, offering its poor farmer's house pretense. We confront two blasphemers; they have no children, no livestock. Against every Hell born contagion and indelible misery and emissary of Satan we encounter, our American Winchester rifles and the torch are tempests that speak for God. I have been at this for four years now. The wind against us, the road against us, Satan's insistent pressures at our throats, at our backs, against our every act, against our every thought and prayer, we ride on—Damnation fire wind. Wind damnation gunfire. No silence. Dust and wind. Upright serpents walking on to feet and customs of evil. Fire and fire. No silence. Crumbling houses and weakness and flames that swirl and plunge into one another. Damnation and darkness, the spread of defects and sin. No silence. Dust and dust and dust. Evil in every face. Miserable every face. Ashes, swept-up and swirling in the wind. Corpses and grotesque monstrosities with the pretense of human faces. Gunfire. No silence. Gunfire. The properties of wickedness put to fire today. Ashes. Wind damning us today. No silence. No rest for us.

Crest of a short hill pocked and striped with water-runoff ruts it took our horses an hour to achieve. Another sin before us. Another abomination.

"From Hell." Sebstiano spits.

"It is," Janning replies.

In the dead rot and cold remains of the grey hollow below us, thrust aloft by short, bent poles, above what a tall man may stretch-up and grasp, on a platform of grey warped boards and twisted sticks, some thick as a small woman's thigh, sits a hut. A hut encircled by makeshift fencing made of bones and antlers. It creaks and groans in the shrieking wind. Topped with old straw, made of boards and pieces of tin, and mud, the lair of a witch, the quintessence of what a godless place looks like.

Janning hissed lowly. "*Baba Yaga.*"

Everything here stained and blemished by Satan's dance, we are in the black districts of her legends.

Barking satanic noise, the gruesome face of the Devil-owned crone erupts from the doorway. The witch has black teeth, they look like sharpened stakes of iron. She is bone-thin. Three American Winchester rifles strike out. She is bleeding, a fallen sack in the dirt. We reload and empty our American Winchester rifles again. Without racing, we put ravenous and all the days of her calendar to the torch. Stand and watch every fiber burn, watch the flames curve, bend and stretch, soar. We ride on in the grey morning, the wind against us, the road against us. Long road. All day. Hard road. All day. All day cold unrelenting wind. Grey the spilled-clouds that will not be dispelled. Grey, every shout  and stone and winter-shadow kissed by the death fragrance of *again* in our path.

My breath is a grey mist. (Another night) sleepless, denied the comforts of rest, and weary, I pull my blanket tighter about me. Dark and cold, never gone in this world. The wind, never gone, will not be silent, not for a moment. There is no room here for the stories my father told me. There is no room here for memories of the warmth of my mother's kitchen, the herbs in her sunlit garden. Sebastiano is sleeping. Names leak out of his mouth; Oeillet, Pedro Civelo, Alice Kyteler, Nemus and Leebo… Irem. His hands twitch. He has borne these dark fits before. He will be sharp in the morning. Our American Winchester rifles will not be silent in the morning.

End of the day's miserable road. Long uneven road, slowed by deep ruts in the track we ride, slowed by the circumstances of mud and rocks. Wet gullies and dry gullies. Long road of dust our horses' hooves threw up, of dust pushed in our faces by the wind. A devastating road, it had too many moments where it demonstrated the full-sore of brutal. No inn—never a sign of hospitality or ease, a small dwelling of grey stones and grey boards that showed its injuries and gnawing poverty. The odors in the air are foul. The sight of the man before us no less. A bent old man (bent by a life of constantly-repeated consequences) told Janning, the three of us could bed-down in the small wooden structure he called a barn. After we put a silver coin in his hand, we did. With three horses (an old black gelding that belonged to the old man and the two of ours that pulled our coach), a noisy goat, and an owl—it examined us for a time and, deciding we were not digestible, or tasty, left for the dark wilds of broad night scented forest. The old man's old dog (the first we had seen in many months) was lucky; he got to slumber inside the shack with the warm-embers of the old man's small fire.

We slept on hay (it was dry), in our coats and hats. The cold held us, we shivered. Janning whispered his irritations, slept with his American Winchester rifle. Outside in the impossibly-thick blackness nothing can cut, horrible sounds, not howls or barks, but unnatural *growlings*, snapped and fell, and sour smells, rotten and blatantly graveish, accompanied them. Janning's white-knuckled hands refused to lessen their grip on his American Winchester rifle and he repeatedly mumbled about the *anderen Wölfe* and *der Weg nach Hause*, and the *Graue Blutegel*.

Break of day. Woke. Deeply chilled, but in one piece. Sat inside by the old man's small fire as it struggled to stand tall. What passed for herb tea. Cheese and a slice of yesterday's bread for each of us. No marmalade no sugar no coffee no eggs.

Brother Sebastiano performed his abrupt task. I assisted Janning in hitching our horses to the coach. We did not turn and look upon the bent old man and his old woman. We burn what we put down and ride on in the grey morning. The wind slaps us—

Another day surrounded by evil things.

There is no room for solace here.

Grey, threatening rain.

Long morning on the road, slowed by the flutterings of this rotted clime that drinks hearts and prayers, and the circumstances of mud and rocks—

I am searching for Rome, for the stories my father told me, for memories of the warmth of my dear mother's kitchen.

"I miss butter…" *and pleasantries exchanged with my good neighbors.*


*(Stereolab & Nurse With Wound "Trippin' With The Birds")*

# About the Author

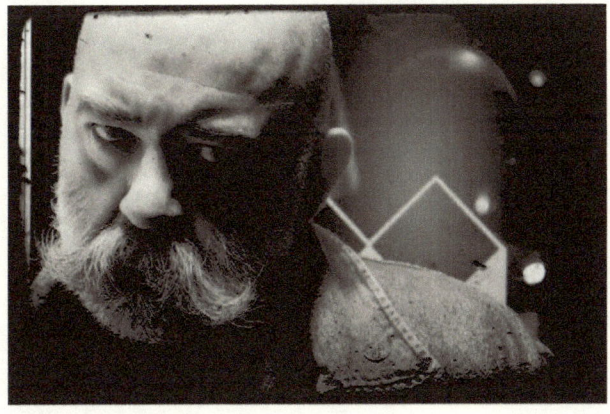

A restless searcher, drawn to mysteries and mystics, devils and nightmares, JoePulverisaMartian, a literary construct composed of other-era junk found in Tom Waits' basement and outtakes from ECM recording sessions. He discovered Lovecraft at 15, fell hard. Discovered (his greatest literary influence) Robert W. Chambers shortly after, fell harder! !! When he began to write in his 40's, Pulver played in fields he loved as a teen. He still does. HPL and Robert W. Chambers are in much of his work (as a writer and an editor), yet it abounds w/ *other* influences as well, *NOIR* (Goodis, Thompson, Ellroy, and Himes), Marvel Comics, poetry (E. E. Cummings, Philip Lamantia), Weird Fiction (Michael Cisco, Jean Ray, Ligotti), and all manner of music. Pulver is not one to shy away from his influences, but they only serve as fingerposts, his work remains 'uniquely his own'.

Joseph S. Pulver, Sr. has released 4 acclaimed mixed-genre collections (*Blood Will Have Its Season, SIN & ashes, Portraits of Ruin, A House of Hollow Wounds*), a collection of King in Yellow tales (*King in Yellow Tales Vol. 1*), 2 weird fiction novels, and he's edited *A Season in Carcosa*, the *Shirley Jackson Award*-winning *The Grimscribe's Puppets, Cassilda's Song*, Ann K. Schwader's *The Worm's Remember*, and *The Doom That Came to Providence* (the 2015 *NecronomiCON Providence* round-robin). His fiction and poetry has appeared in many notable anthologies, including *Autumn Cthulhu, The Children of Old Leech*, Ellen Datlow's *The Year's Best Horror, The Book of Cthulhu, A Mountain Walked*, and *Best Weird Fiction of the Year*. Joe is a regular contributor to the *Lovecraft eZine*.

# ALSO FROM

# LOVECRAFT EZINE PRESS

www.ingramcontent.com/pod-product-compliance
Lightning Source LLC
Chambersburg PA
CBHW020611130626
46552CB00007B/3150